THE MOST BEAUTIFUL
TREE IN THE WORLD

by Leonard Weisgard

WONDER BOOKS • NEW YORK
A Division of GROSSET & DUNLAP, Inc.

"Andy! A-n-d-y!" Ellen stopped in the yard and waited for an answer from her brother. Suddenly a shower of snow fell upon her head.

She turned toward the large spruce tree behind her and saw Andy peering between the drooping

branches. She scooped up a mittenful of snow and chased after him. Round and round the tree they ran, laughing and shouting so gaily that they didn't hear the humming motor till it was directly overhead. Then they looked up to see what was there.

"Oh, boy!" cried Andy. "A helicopter! A real one!"

The helicopter circled the giant evergreen twice and then headed toward New York, whose sky-scrapers were far beyond the hills.

Andy and Ellen raced to the house, where their father was waiting for them at the door.

"Daddy! Daddy!" shouted Andy. "We just saw a helicopter! It flew right around our big spruce."

"What do you suppose it was doing?" asked Ellen.

"Well, it's hard to say, children. Let's talk about it while we eat dinner," their father said. He was taking care of them while their mother was in the hospital. In a few days she would come home with a new baby brother for Andy and Ellen.

As they sat down at the table, their father asked,
"Now, what's this about a helicopter?"

"I think the man in the helicopter just wanted to
look at our big tree because it's so beautiful," Ellen
said. "It's like a great big Christmas tree, isn't it?"

"It may look like a Christmas tree," Andy answered quickly, but it will never be one, because we're not ever going to cut it down. Right, Daddy?"

"I don't think there's much danger of its ever becoming a Christmas tree," Andy's father reassured him. "It's too large. Besides, we all love it too much."

Just then the telephone rang. A few minutes later,
their father came back. "Well, Ellen," he said, "you
were right. The man in the helicopter was admiring
our tree. He called to say that he wants to buy it."

"You didn't sell it, did you?" Andy asked.

"No, son, I didn't sell it. And we won't, either, unless we all agree that's what we want to do. I told the man to come out tomorrow and talk to us about it."

"In his helicopter, Dad?"

"Yes, Andy. It will land right in back of the house."

When the children came home from school the
next day, the helicopter was landing in the pasture.
As the pilot climbed out, he called, "Hi, there!"

The children rushed up to greet the pilot. Then
their father came along, too, and said, "Well, Mr.
Judson, as I told you last night, we think we have
the most beautiful tree in the world. Nothing can
make us sell it unless there is a good reason for it."

"I can understand that, Mr. Brooks," the pilot answered. "Have you told the children why I want to buy it?"

"No. I've left that for you."

"Well," said the pilot to Andy and Ellen, "I want to buy it for a Christmas tree—a special Christmas tree, to be set up in Rockefeller Center in New York —for everyone to enjoy. What do you think now?"

"What's Rockefeller Center?" asked Ellen.

"Oh, I know!" cried Andy. "That's where we went last year to see the great big tree that was all covered with colored lights. Don't you remember, Ellen?"

"Where the people were ice-skating down below the tree? Oh, yes! It was so beautiful!"

Mr. Judson smiled and said, "Just think, Ellen. More than a million people will see your tree at Rockefeller Center. Nearly fifty million people will

see it on television. You'll see it, too, and share it with them. But it will still be your tree, because you're the only ones who have watched it grow."

Ellen looked at Andy and Andy looked at her. Then they both looked at their father. Andy said, "Well, Daddy, we agree—if you and Mother do, too."

"We agree," Mr. Brooks said. "The tree really has lived the best years of its life with us, and we should be ready to share it with others."

The next day a crew of men started cutting down
the big evergreen. They attached a cable high on
the trunk so the crane could lower the tree gently.
They trussed up the branches so that none would be

crushed. Then they put the tree on a big truck, tied it down with ropes and drove away.

Andy and Ellen were sad, at first, to see the tree go. But they knew they would love seeing their tree in Rockefeller Center.

Finally, the great day came! The children climbed excitedly into the car to drive to the city with their father. It was a long ride, and a cold one. But when they stood on the sidewalk, looking up at their great tree and the many lights it had all over it, nothing else mattered.

Their father took them to see the tree again the next day. They loved looking at their stupendous Christmas tree, and watching the skaters below. They loved seeing other people admire the tree. And they liked watching an artist paint it. But when they got home, they felt a little sad to see only an empty space where the big spruce had been.

Then, two days before Christmas, there was something even more exciting to think about. Mother was coming home!

Andy met her at the door.

"Hi, Mommy!" he called excitedly. "I'm so glad you're home. Did you bring the baby?"

Ellen was close at his heels, but both stopped short as their mother let them see what she was carrying in her arms. "Here he is," she said smiling. "Your

baby brother!" They all gathered around the sleep-
ing baby.

Then their father said, "And now I have a surprise
for you all. Look outside!"

Ellen ran to the window.

"Oh, Andy, come quick! Look, Mother!" shouted
Ellen. "Some men have brought a little evergreen
tree! And they're planting it in our yard—near where
the big one was!"

Everyone hurried to the window. Mr. Brooks
smiled at the puzzled look on his children's faces.
"You see," he explained, "when I sold the spruce to
Mr. Judson, he promised to plant a new tree in its
place. It, too, may grow up to be one of the most
beautiful trees in the world!"

"It already is," said Andy and Ellen happily as they
looked at the little tree standing in the yard.